"Pawsitive Pals

Written by: Angela O'Toole

Illustrated by: Bianca Truncali

AuthorHouse™
1663 Liberty Drive
Bloomington, IN 47403
www.authorhouse.com
Phone: 1 (800) 839-8640

Published by AuthorHouse 12/29/2017

ISBN: 978-1-5462-2317-7 (sc)
ISBN: 978-1-5462-2316-0 (e)

Library of Congress Control Number: 2017919748

Print information available on the last page.

Any people depicted in stock imagery provided by Thinkstock are models,
and such images are being used for illustrative purposes only.
Certain stock imagery © Thinkstock.

This book is printed on acid-free paper.

authorHOUSE®

Dedications and Acknowledgements

This book is dedicated to the memory of our canine friends Darla, Pugsley, Oscar, Rocky, Zeppy, Calamity, and Jellybean. We miss you terribly and love you!

This book is also dedicated to Bernadine Iaccarino, a truly wonderful friend to us. Bianca, Nathan, and I would like to thank our fans for their continued support as we look to reach children on issues that are present in school and society.

This book was written in loving memory of Casta Miskowitz.

"One day, you just wait, squirrels, I will finally catch you," promised Nate. "Hey, Doug, where were you when I needed you to teach these squirrels a lesson?" questioned Nate. Speaking of lesson, Doug was there to walk to the bus stop so they wouldn't be late for class at their schools. Nate attends Top Dog Elementary School while Doug goes to Feline A"Cat"emy. Suddenly, Nate started "coughing" and walked wearily back home. Nate was going to be out "sick" again. That would make four days in a row. Doug thought something was fishy about Nate's behavior. As Doug boarded the bus with his "cat"mates, Reggie and Boots, he pondered what to do.

Ms. Fusco called attendance and once Nate didn't bark when his name was said, his classmates looked at each other in dismay. "Does anyone know what is wrong with Nathan?", asked Ms. Fusco. "We have our big test coming in two weeks and he is really missing a lot." "I did see him at the park yesterday and he seemed to be the picture of health," stated Mittens. "Maybe he got sick after the park," suggested Speedy. Nate's pupmates decided to visit Nate that day.

Nate was sunning himself, belly up, in the window when some of his friends surprised him. He quickly jumped into his robe and grabbed the tissue box. "Nate, buddy, what's wrong?" asked Mittens. "We miss you in school and will help you with all the work you are missing," explained Ruby. Nate looked the least bit interested and changed the subject to the latest squeaky toy he received. The moment school was mentioned, it was as if the cat had Nate's tongue.

"I hope Nate comes in tomorrow. Class isn't the same without him," whimpered Jackson. "Yeah, he always has the best snacks during lunchtime," chimed in Jake. Some of Nate's friends weren't convinced that he in fact was "sick". Jameson and Bailey decided to get to the bottom of it. Together, with Gizmo and Betsy, the foursome headed to Nate's.

On the way over, they met up with Jax, Yogi, and Rascal and the crew made a bee line to Nate's house. They were surprised to see most of the class outside Nate's door. Nate, "coughing" and sluggish, made his way outside. "Hey, guys, what's going on?" inquired Nate. Layla presented Nate with important notes he missed the days he was out. Putting them quickly aside, Nate said he would look at them later. "Thanks for checking on me but I must go and rest," said Nathan.

Nate's mom decided it was time for a vet visit. Even she thought it was "paws"ible that Nate was pulling her leg. As the doctor examined him, he discovered something interesting. Each time the word "test" was mentioned, Nathan would shake and put his tail between his legs. To be on the safe side, Dr. Gastaldi called in his assistants, Jasper, Jax, and Bailey. The Lab and cats were ordered to perform some exams on Nate. Once they were completed and the results came back, everyone was even more perplexed. The "lab" report and "cat scan" didn't show anything unusual.

The doctor decided to talk to Nathan alone and asked a plethora of questions. Upon further investigation, the vet came to a conclusion and diagnosed Nathan with a case of test anxiety. The upcoming exam he is supposed to take next week has made Nathan as sick as a dog. The remedy suggested was to surround Nate with his "paws"itive pals to help him work through this issue. The friends put their heads together to devise a plan.

Chloe and Sandy decided to coax Nathan back to school with the perfect method! They lined the street to school with "squirrels" knowing that Nathan would run up to each one and eventually end up in his classroom. The morning came and everything went as planned. Nate sprinted up to each "squirrel", investigated it, realized it was a fake, and went on to the next. Nate made his way to Top Dog Elementary School much to his displeasure.

All of Nathan's friends and Ms. Fusco were waiting for him. "I can't take the stress of the test! Please let me go home!" pleaded Nate. "Don't stress the test!" Ms. Fusco stated. "A test is just a test. What you do in class on a daily basis allows me to really see if you mastered the skills taught." Artie went up to Nathan, put his paw on his shoulder and said, "You see, so what we told you all along is true." "Yes, there is no need to get stressed out so much that you made yourself sick. If you do all the work each day and try your best, you will be successful. One test doesn't determine everything," stated Simba.

Nate sat there, surrounded by his pals, and finally came to understand the reason for "the BIG test". It is meant to determine the academic growth of each student from the previous year. The teachers use the results as a small piece of the picture of the whole student. After this "pup"talk, Nate changed his tune about school. Of course, Nate will put his best paw forward on that test and every one he will take in the future but it will no longer be the reason to keep him from attending school.

The day of the test was upon the pups. One by one, they listened to commands and performed what was asked. It was Nate's turn. He strutted into the room, head held high and was attentive to the words of Ms. Fusco. With each request, Nate aced one after the next and his confidence built. Once it was over, a weight was lifted off his shoulders. He and his pals shared a treat in celebration.

The results were in and Nathan's score was off the charts! Sumo, Bella, and Harrison, Nate's "fur"ever friends, went by his house to congratulate him. Nate told them he had learned a great lesson Don't stress the test! He became the poster dog promoting his message to all kids – "Think "Paws"itive because you're "Paw"fect!" Nate went on a tour through the United States and even got his own star on the Hollywood Walk of Fame. As Nate got a taste of "pup"ularity, he thought about what his future could hold. At that moment, his mom's phone rang…….

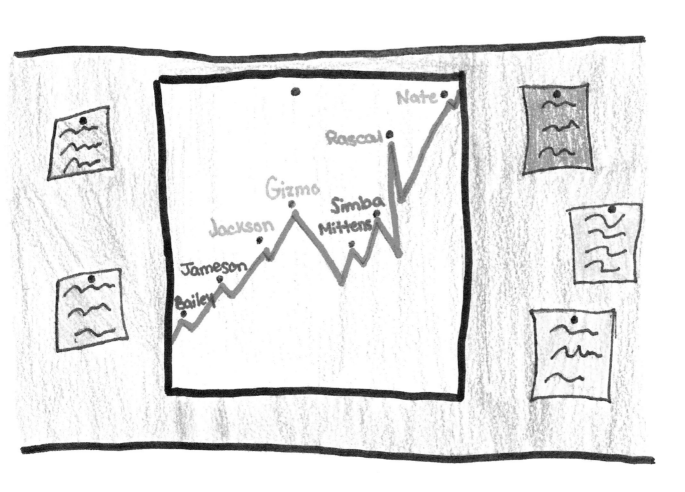

Paw-sitive Airplane Inc.

Nate's mom hung up the phone and exclaimed, "Pack your bags. Your story has spread like wildfire. Hollywood is calling." In the blink of an eye, Nate's life was about to become very different. Flight 626 to California was ready for take-off and there, sitting in First Class, was Nathan! What is the first stop? The *Ellen Show,* of course! As he exited the plane, his fans went bananas and filled the air with a"paws". Nathan looked up at his mom and knew this could be the start of something wonderful.

To be continued….

Angela T. O'Toole is a 5th grade teacher at PS 30 in Staten Island, NY. This is the second book written by Angela T. O'Toole and illustrated by Bianca Truncali. Bianca was a 5th grade student in Angela's class and upon graduation, they teamed up to form a partnership to get important messages across to children worldwide. Angela was aware of Bianca's artistic abilities and was thrilled to have her illustrate the words she wrote. The focus of Angela's work centers around topics found within schools that children experience. Nathan, Angela's 6 year old Dachshund, is the main character of both books. Angela, Bianca, and Nathan will continue their work in a third book coming soon featuring new puppy pals. They make a "paw"fect team!

CPSIA information can be obtained
at www.ICGtesting.com
Printed in the USA
BVOW07s0620130218
507891BV00013B/27/P